A Special Kind of Sister

A SPECIAL
KIND OF SISTER

by Lucia B. Smith
illustrated by Chuck Hall

Holt, Rinehart and Winston / *New York*

Text copyright © 1977, 1979 by Lucia B. Smith
Illustrations copyright © 1977, 1979 by Chuck Hall
All rights reserved, including the right to reproduce
this book or portions thereof in any form.
Published simultaneously in Canada by Holt, Rinehart
and Winston of Canada, Limited.
Printed in the United States of America
10   9   8   7   6   5   4   3   2   1

Library of Congress Cataloging in Publication Data

Smith, Lucia B.
  A special kind of sister.

  SUMMARY: A young girl describes her
relationship with her brain-damaged brother.
  [1. Brain-damaged children — Fiction.
2. Mentally handicapped — Fiction. 3. Brothers
and sisters — Fiction] I. Hall, Chuck.
II. Title.
PZ7.S6545Sp   [E]   78-14096
ISBN 0-03-047121-4

To Kirsten,
a daughter, a sister,
a person—all special.

A Special Kind of Sister

My name is Sarah. I'm 7 and ¼ years old. I have a Mom and a Dad and a brother, Andy. We are a very special family.

You see, Andy is different. He'll always be different.

It's not easy having a brother who is retarded. But we are trying to make it into a good thing instead of a bad thing.

Andy is only 5. But I remember that he was a baby for such a long time. He still can't do much. My Dad said, "That's the way he came. That's the way he is."

Someday I'll be a doctor or a teacher, but Andy will never be able to do those things. Those people will be helping him.

Something is always going wrong with Andy. He either hurts himself or gets real sick. I wonder why I'm always O.K. Oh, once I had to get four stitches on my chin. But that was no big deal. With all that is the matter with him, I could get hurt or sick once in a while. I wouldn't mind.

Besides, then they would have to forget about Andy for a while and take care of me.

How come I have to make my bed and set the table? How come I'm the one who has to do homework and get good grades?

When Andy learned to use a spoon, everybody oohed and aahed. Big deal!

I know it's hard for Andy, but I'm trying so hard—for them.

In the summer, I go to Andy's school. We have the most fun there.

At first, I felt bad that Andy couldn't do a puzzle some of the others were doing. But I helped him and he tried so hard. Now he can do that puzzle.

When a girl there was making fun of Andy, I hit her. But the teacher said, "Andy is not like a hurt bird. Let him learn to take care of himself."

I don't want anyone else to hurt Andy.

Last night I had a dream. It was like a nightmare. I was dreaming that what happened to Andy happened to me.

We were at a restaurant and Mom had to feed me. And I didn't look right.

People were staring at me, and boys and girls were laughing. It was worse than a monster dream.

I told my Mom about it. We both cried.

I'm sure lucky to be Sarah.

I told my Mom that I was glad that I wasn't Andy.
She said, "I'm glad that you're you, too."

The fair was awful. Andy didn't have any fun. Mom and Dad didn't. And neither did I. People whispered and stared and pointed. Andy couldn't go on many rides. The noises scared him. We tried to have fun. But it didn't work. Next time Mom and Dad said we will go all by ourselves.

I think Andy will have a good time with the babysitter.

Sometimes I wake up and say, "Please be a good day. Please Andy, keep all your yells inside today."

I hate it when he makes Mom so cranky. It makes me feel cold and dark inside. I stay by myself. But I don't want to.

That Andy. He's a real troublemaker.

Later my Mom says we were all mad today. But it's not bad to be mad. We'll make tomorrow better.

My best friend Carrie and I were at the park with Andy. He was tugging at a man's coat. The man turned around and said, "What's the matter with that kid?"

I looked for my Dad, but he was too far away. So, I puffed myself up and said, "Well, he's retarded and he can't talk. But I think he's trying to tell you that he likes you."

The man left.

I was so scared. Carrie squeezed my hand tight. She understands.

But everybody doesn't understand.

I remember the day Marianne came over. She couldn't even look at Andy. She got mad and told me she had to go. She didn't want to play with a "weirdo." My Mom told me that Marianne was scared and she didn't know any better.

But I sure didn't have any new friends over for a long time. I still don't like to.

I have an important job. It's not easy, but I'm really good at it.

I'm helping Andy with his exercises. I'm like a teacher — and Andy is learning to get stronger.

It's too bad that Andy can't do all the things I can do. He must feel bad about it.

It's good to know he needs me.

Carrie and I had a big fight today. We called each other names and I came home feeling sick inside.

Andy started tagging around after me. He can really be a pest sometimes.

But when I sat down, Andy gave me the biggest hug. And we just sat together like that for a long time.

I was feeling better.

Andy really cares. He must love me a lot.

About the Author

Lucia B. Smith was born and raised in New York, graduated from Rosemont College in Pennsylvania, and has a master's degree in Early Childhood Education from La Verne College in California. She lives with her husband, Peter, and their two daughters in southern California.

About the Illustrator

Chuck Hall, whose works have been exhibited throughout the Southwest, has been an art teacher as well as a professional illustrator. He lives in Diamond Bar, California.

DATE DUE			
MAY			

362.4
Smi   Smith, Lucia B.

AUTHOR

A special kind of sister

TITLE

DATE DUE	BORROWER'S NAME	ROOM NUMBER
MAY 78	Krista	C-2
	Logue	7
DEC 18 '85	Parker	

362.4
Smi

Smith, Lucia B.

A special kind of sister